Lola
#2

Lola's SUPER CLUB

"My Substitute Teacher is a Witch"

PAPERCUTZ™
NEW YORK

MORE GREAT GRAPHIC NOVEL SERIES AVAILABLE FROM PAPERCUTZ™

THE SMURFS TALES

THE ONLY LIVING GIRL

BRINA THE CAT

THE SISTERS

CAT & CAT

ASTRO MOUSE AND LIGHT BULB

ASTERIX

GERONIMO STILTON REPORTER

DINOSAUR EXPLORERS

GEEKY FAB 5

FUZZY BASEBALL

THE MYTHICS

MAGICAL HISTORY TOUR

THE LITTLE MERMAID

SCHOOL FOR EXTRATERRESTRIAL GIRLS

GILLBERT

THE LOUD HOUSE

MELOWY

ATTACK OF THE STUFF

GUMBY

papercutz.com
Also available as ebooks wherever ebooks are sold.

Lola's SUPER CLUB

2 - "MY SUBSTITUTE TEACHER IS A WITCH"

Script and art
Christine Beigel + Pierre Fouillet

Original editors
Maxi Luchini + Ed

Original designer
Immaculada Bordell

Paperback ISBN: 978-1-5458-0636-4
Hardcover ISBN: 978-1-5458-0635-7

Special thanks to Stephanie Barrouillet, Xavier Belltrán,
and Patricia Montalbán

Papercutz books may be purchased for business or promotional use.
For information on bulk purchases please contact
Macmillan Corporate and Premium Sales Department at
(800) 221-795 x5442.

Jeff Whitman – Translator, Letterer, Production, Editor
Jim Salicrup
Editor-in-Chief

Printed in China
August 2021

First Papercutz Printing
Distributed by Macmillan

PREVIOUSLY IN LOLA'S SUPER CLUB, LOLA (IN HER TUTU) AND HER SUPER CLUB, HER STUFFED DINO WITH A GROWTH SPURT PROBLEM, JAMES (IN UNDIES) AND HER CAT HOT DOG (IN DENIAL), HAD TO RESCUE HER HAPLESS DAD -- WHO IS ALSO SUPER SECRET AGENT JAMES BLOND -- FROM MAX IMUM AND HIS HENCH-DOGS ZERO + ZERO.

ALONG THE WAY, OUR HEROES MET THE SHAPE-CHANGING SCRIBBLE MONSTER MOMINA, A LIVELY SKELETON COUPLE WHO WERE ONCE SPIES, A SUPER-SHARK, AND A CROC WHO THINKS NOTHING IS FAIR. NOT TO MENTION THE FABLED PIRATE CAPTAIN RAIN-BEARD, THE VINE-SWINGING JUNGLOR, AND THE HIGH-FLYING SUPER HERO MOD MAN! TRULY A SUPER CLUB!

BUT MAX IMUM HAS MAXIMUM HELP TOO FROM HIS FAMILY, THE WICKED SPELL-CASTER MINI MUM AND HER RICH (BUT FORGETTABLE) LOVER, PRINCE GUINEMO, SORRY, GUILLERMO, (HIS NAME IS SO FORGETTABLE). WITH THE TWO CLUBS FORMED, IT'S UP TO LOLA'S SUPER CLUB TO SAVE HER HOMETOWN OF FRIENDLY FALLS AND EVERYONE IN IT... ONE ADVENTURE AT A TIME!

Lola's SUPER CLUB

SCHOOL

No way!

You brought it?

Show us! Show us!

Everyone ready?

Go on, LOLA!

Tah-dah!

¿Pff...¿

I thought it was going to be a project on hot dogs...

It's about SUPER HOT DOG of Friendly Falls...

Is it a cat made out of hot dogs?

Can I eat him? ¿Uff,¿ smells yummy!

RING RING RING RING

7

Coats on their hooks!

I don't have a coat, what do I do, ma'am?

INSIDE NOW! LET'S GO! Huh? How? What's on your head?

Ah, I see you use a super hold gel! Don't move so much, you look like a piñata... Don't fret, I'll be back soon...

SPLOSH

TO YOUR SEATS! And siiiiiiiiiiiiiilence!

If you continue behaving like this, I'll be forced to punish you. Nyuk nyuk...

How strange! This teacher reminds me of someone...

POP QUIZ!

Knock Knock Knock

I said don't move out there, wiggly gelatin boy!

It's me, Mommy!

Oh! Come in, come in...

MAX IMUM!

Even as a kid, he's ridiculous!

What a stache!

Look! Did you see? He's not bald!

Shh...

It has to be a wig.

I've always wanted to wear one. One day...

Shush!

Who spoke out?

Don't just stand there, Max. Go sit.

Where, Ma-- uh, Miss?

Next to the girl in the tutu! Get! What's your name, dear?

Lola.

Very well, Lola...

Eh... A mattress salesman? No? A one-hit wonder? I'm sure he isn't a football star, I know all of them...

I know! I know! A professor who works at Racula College.

Racula? Where's that?

It's a city in Poland.

Dracula is from Romania! Wrong answer! And when someone's wrong...

AAAAAH!

WRAK

WRAK

MOM!

CLAC

CLAC

Who else wants a try? C'mon, let's go, kids... participation counts.

You!

Me?

12

Yes, cream puff. I'll give you a hint. Nyuk! Dracula's a count and his favorite color is red.

Is it the nickname of Little Red Riding Hood?

Wrong answer! Trap door!

You're a witch!

Mommy! I mean, teacher... Lola said that...!

Ow!

No one likes a tattletale, Max...

Well, I see you don't know the horrors of this world.

NYiiiC

Seems so! You're absolutely right, teacher.

What do they teach in school these days?

Hey, mister! Our Costume Day isn't today, it's next Monday.

Wow! Your fake teeth are really cool! They seem real.

To the trap door!

!

We have to do something. If this keeps up, the whole class will disappear.

Lola, want to share with the rest of the class?

No... but, may I go to the bathroom?

Mmm... You have one minute, I'm timing you!

14

* It's whatshisface! Guinemo? See LOLA'S SUPER CLUB #1

Huh. Is the book any good?

Wow! It's you! Super-Lola!

Read this, sticky slug!

SPLASH

Don't forget to flush... Adios, goop!

FRiiiiSH

--la!

Hey!

Well, well... Look who's back. I thought Costume Day was next Monday...

Laugh, witch. I'll stop you soon enough!

We'll see about that. And call me "teacher"!

GRRRR!

Anywho! In your absence, there's been...

...a marathon of wrong answers.

And as we had some empty desks, our friend Vlad Dracula brought in three new students.

Wolf Man...

...Fiery Dragon...

...and Rocky Ogre!

Hiya, kids!

Ha! Two can play at this game...

Super Club, to your seats!

You'll see!

Fear, give a deadly fright, goose bumps...

You, next to Lola. Read a page of the Spellbook of the Bag Witches.

Well, it's just...

We don't have that book.

Then use mine! But be careful! It's very valuable.

MOMINA!

Got it!

What page?

1313.

1256...1299...

Well? We don't have all day.

Here! Page 1313! Macabre laugh potion...

Classic witchcraft... Continue.

To prepare a magical potion for who--

...who-hoo...

Good!

You need a big cauldron, dust of a me-te-o...

Very good!

Dust of a meteorite!

NEXT!

You! The fake fish with scales and big teeth.

Me? It's not fair.

You need a big cauldron, dust of a meteorite...

What else?

...a good chunk of ...Huh? Oh, no! Of stern... sterno...

...cleido...

...mastoid...

I heard you! No blabbing!

...terno... sternocleido...

Got it! I know! Sterno-cleidomastoid!

Very good... I saw that, Shark... Punished!

TO THE TRAP DOOOOR!

Honestly, this doesn't smell all that great.

What did they bring us? A shark! Robotoc, get this chum out of my stew!

Me-chum-do-what-with?

Bring it to GLUTBOOG!

Glut-what? A bit of respect! I'm no chum!

Lola's friends! Keep calm, the Super Club will save you!

What's this? I only cook with organic boogers!

Boss-say-chum-bring-to-Glutboog. Say-Glutboog-like-chum.

That won't do. Gotta be organic. Look at these boogers here, so fresh... 100% biological. What you bring me is transgenic!

Me-Robot-Bionic-obey-orders-chef-Karlos-Fantonato-13.

You-leave-now!

I'm misunderstood. No one values my culinary arts. But you know what I'm talking about, right, boogers?

Yes... Cry, cry... More runny noses. 100% biological beautiful boogers!

Meanwhile, in class...

...remove from heat, add the sternocleidomastoid, hairs of an oxidized witch and...

Enough!

You seem ready, huh? See if you can calculate this then!

$$\frac{0+0+0+0+0-0^2}{0} \times 00 = ?$$

Math! Sum it up!

No-brainer.

The ogre's head! Void!

Boo-Hoo!

What? Villains don't cry! Ever! Get to the board, Ogre!

Tell me the result, balance the equation.

Zero!

What? I failed? But, teach!

Sigh! Take your seat, hurry. It's almost recess!

Can't, I'm stuck...

RING

For once she tells the truth.

I can confirm.

I will never understand kids...

What did you say? Share it with the rest of the class.

Huh? It's just... Well, on Mondays we have presentations.

Yes, yes, yes. Max, go do yours now.

About what? Villains? About that, Mom?

Go ahead, dearie. We're listening.

Villains... Villains are... villains.

Louder!

Villains are very, very, very villainous. To be even more villainous than very, very, very, villainous they eat villainously. The villainous vampire drinks the blood of good children. The villainous ogre eats good children. The villainous wolf man scares the parents of good children. And, the more good people there are on the planet, the more villainous the villains get.

Bravo, my dear! A round of applause! I said applause!

Not so fast! You forgot a small... No! A big detail.

Oh, yeah! Ghostly villains scare good children and their parents at home.

Cold.

Zombie villains devour the brains of good children?

Colder!

Should I warm up your mind?

But...

Or barbecue you? Which is it?

Of course! Max Imum, I know. Dragon villains set fire to bag witches' brooms to char their butts. Their kids' butts too!

That's extremely villainous... Mommy!

It wasn't me! He started it.

But it was the truth.

Dragon, to the trap door!

I hate school!

Max, you get an A. But you, Super Lola, should avoid the trap door... But I'm curious. Let's see what you got...

For my presentation, I will teach you all about... hot dogs! I present to you... Friendly Falls' own Super Hot Dog!

Super Hot Dog can do anything.

He's an expert at arithmetic and in geometry, he's great. He also knows a ton of geography. And he can find the most remote areas on a map like Minachina, Babia, a country-quite-far, the Moon of Memphis, the tenth wonder of the world, Atlantis, and El Dorodo. All with his eyes closed!

He's the best hot dog in the world. Anyone who knows him is hooked.

And also he's a lover of the arts, in all its forms. Sketching, painting, collage, knitting, video editing, music, and even interpretive dance. It's all art to him! Even in the kitchen, which is his true strength.

And his name! He isn't Super Hot Dog just because. It's his favorite dish.

Have a question about the environment? Want to know something in particular about the living world, be it animals or plants? Or the dead? Or about extraterrestrials? Ask Super Hot Dog! He knows everything about everything. He knows all stories, real and fiction, like the back of his paw.

He's the best at handwriting. He never makes grammatical mistakes and can recite the most difficult poems without stopping or messing up.

For example: "Sausages are sausaged with sauce and scrap. Who shall sausage the sausage? The sausage strolls soundly south on the shelf shaping said sausage sufficiently."

Want to try, teach?

Huh? What?

Well... Good. Good, good, good.

It's noon! Now it's... ⸮Ahem!⸍ ⸮Ahem!⸍

Everyone to Lunch!

Teacher! I don't have a lunch pass...

Don't you worry, my poisoned apple. The school pays today.

I hope you're all hungry, because the chef has prepared a menu good for indigestion...

CAFE ERIA

That's why I never eat at school. I'm allergic!

Relax, my pretty. If anyone has an allergy today... Nyuk! Nyuk... it's me... To students! Nyuk!

Why are you laughing?

Silence! Let's see... Where was I? Oh, yeah! We only cook with the freshest products. Don't worry about allergies, yogurt cup.

Yogurt? I can't eat that, Ma'am. Yogurt has milk!

If you keep it up, kid, I'm going to send you right home...! There's an allergy for you!

That clear? Read the menu, go on!

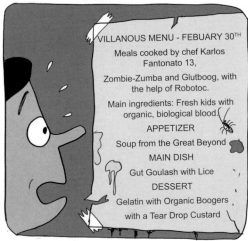
VILLANOUS MENU - FEBUARY 30TH

Meals cooked by chef Karlos Fantonato 13,

Zombie-Zumba and Glutboog, with the help of Robotoc.

Main ingredients: Fresh kids with organic, biological blood.

APPETIZER

Soup from the Great Beyond

MAIN DISH

Gut Goulash with Lice

DESSERT

Gelatin with Organic Boogers with a Tear Drop Custard

Terrified kids and sea life stewed in fresh blood... A family recipe, you'll see.

First, I boil the living-dead kids. This way, the guts fall right out with the arm. You don't even need a fork!

Gelatin and Tear Drop Custard... A delicate combination of sweet and salty.

Boogers from kids, all organic! Green, liquidy, and sweet too. And for the custard, a generous helping of salty tears.

No pushing! There's enough for everyone! Respect the line...

Just a minute, bag witch?

"Teacher"! It's not that hard!

Forgetting something?

At this school, the kids pick the menu!

Huh? What? The principal doesn't say so.

Well, it was the principal's idea!

The principal's? Nyuk! Nyuk! Let's ask him. The more, the miserable.

Dearie? Come here!

33

Coming, coming...

Principal Prince Guillermo, we want a food fight!

Huh...? I mean, um... Well... I...

Quiet, pretty boy.

You made a villainous menu out of Kids. Good job.

And we want to put villains on the menu.

And you'll be the judge. Deal?

Deal... No! Wait, wait! What's the prize?

The right to live!

Nyuk! How naive... Deal.

Listen up, Super Club!

Sharpen the knives! Turn on the ovens and heat the oil! Ready!

CH 13

Help us, Max Imum. Come on!

CHAC
CHAC
CHAC

Max! What are you doing? Come here right now or I'll put you in the Soup of the Day!

But, Mommy, for once I'd like to cook some villains...

SHROC
SHROC

Ziiiiiiii

GOLOUP
GOLOUP

PFIOUUU

SUPER-SHARK! There you are! You look a bit seasick! Ha ha! It's a joke, a play on words. Get it?

GLACK!

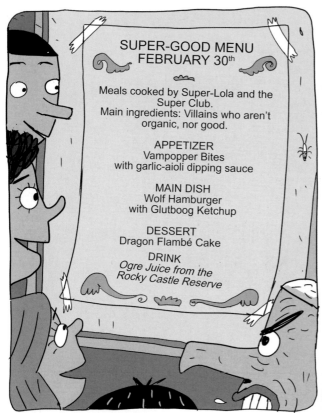

**SUPER-GOOD MENU
FEBRUARY 30th**

Meals cooked by Super-Lola and the Super Club.
Main ingredients: Villains who aren't organic, nor good.

APPETIZER
Vampopper Bites
with garlic-aioli dipping sauce

MAIN DISH
Wolf Hamburger
with Glutboog Ketchup

DESSERT
Dragon Flambé Cake

DRINK
*Ogre Juice from the
Rocky Castle Reserve*

Hello, ladies and gentlemen! To continue we will bring out the plates to see who will be crowned Top-Super-Chef!

If you want the Super Club to win, vote "YES." If you want the villains victorious, vote "NO."

The jury is formed by the most villainous foodies in the world! Give 'em a big boo?

BOO!

On the left... The cream of the crop!

On the right... No comment! First round...and begin!

Terrible...

Dreadful.

Not much consistency!

Yes, very dry.

Enough already! No need to rub salt on my wounds!

An F!

It's not fair.

You try it, dearie.

Are you sure?

I said try it!

¡Gulp!

Ow! It has a strong bite to it!

Flavor's very important. It's to die for!

An F!

Ma'am...

Dearie!

Me again? No way!

What do you say, dearie?

Mmm...

An F!

Let's try the villainous ones...

Let's see... My dear Karlos Fantonato 13, the soup is perfect as always. A ghastly surprise again!

CH13

⊹Gulp!⊹ A+.

Hmm... The goulash is tender, the lice is crisp... In a word...

BRAVO!

⊹Burp!⊹ A+.

Oh! Boogers! How exquisite! And the tears... just the right saltiness. Plus the jiggly gelatin, like the worm's kiss... Perfect consistency of childrens' sadness. Splendid!

⊹BLERG!⊹ ⊹GAH!⊹ ⊹GAH!⊹

The results... Dearie, do you have the summary?

Yeah The Superpeppino... Presentation: Zero+ Consistency: Zero + Taste: Zero = A plate of super-zeroes!

Not bad... Very good! And the villains?

Max score!

$10 + 10 + 100\%$ delicious= ?

Yes, Mom?

Not you, dummy!

Great. Then... Your time's up.

Not so fast, witchie-pie!

40

Hmm... How about we make the leaning Tower of Pisa?

Sure, a tower of pizza!

Hot Dog!

Quick, quick! We have to finish the tower of pizza!

Pisa.

Lisa?

Pisa!

Pizza?

Teressa!

Visa!

Tongue twister!

It's Lisa!

PI-SA!

Tower of pizza?

No, of Visa!

What happened?

Huh...?

Oops!

Now what?

I know what we can do. Huddle up...

Meanwhile, on the villain's dark side...

I propose we do the Tower of Babel.

It's twisted but it'll hold...

Hold it....

Oh, no!

I knew it! Let's try the Tower of Long Ta.

Oh, yeah? And what form is the Tower of Long Ta? Don't tell me, a Dragon?

Well, yes, Mr. Count.. It's a dragon tower..

DLING
NG DLONG
BLING DLANG
BLONG
VG
G

DLING GLING
BLING
BLONG

CLING

It will end up a sleeping tower!

Tic toc, tic toc! Time's running out.

Now, the crucial moment. The scientific part, Dragon?

You're up.

Yesss, Teach!

FFOOUCH

You lost!

Not fair. Our Eiffel Tower was perfect.

That breaks the rules but... okay. If you want to do it your way, we'll do the same...

Super-James in undies!

BONG

Tah-dah, we won.

Obligatory recess. Everyone outtttt!

45

What do you think she's up to? The rain dance?

Stay alert.

¡Psst!

Hi, Lola...

Careful! He's the witch's son!

Let me talk to him...

May I jump rope with you guys?

...29...

YAHOOO! YAHOO!

...99...

Might I know what you're doing?

Hundred!

Max! You want to jump? Very well!

PHYS. ED!

Now we are going to have a physical education class. Very good! This is a bomb. You must throw it to attack. If the ball hits you... you're a prisoner. Or even worse: zombies, vampires, and ogres! Nyuk!

Bag witch! You'll see who's the champs at dodge ball.

TWEE

The first grade
teacher!

The cafeteria chef!

SPLOUCH

The art
teacher!

The second grade teacher!

SPLTOUTCH

The third grade teacher!

And you, Wolf Man? Who are you?

SPLICH

The principal! Sorry! I didn't mean to--

Oh!

SPLOCH

My teacher! At last!

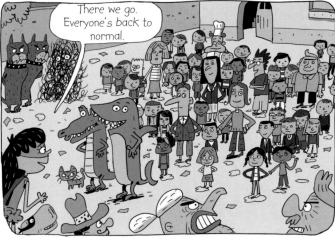

There we go. Everyone's back to normal.

50

So? Who won in the end?

The Kids!

Stuff it, short stuff! Quiet, quiet, quiet! This is all your fault!

RING RING
RING RING

RING

Already? Grr. With your foolishness, I forgot to stop the clock.

RING RING

That was us. We sped up the clock a bit...

Our bones are tired.

Let's go, son! Come on! Call your mutts!

What will I do with you? You don't make a good villain one bit! You embarass the family! Dumb, pathetic boy.

But I just wanted to have fun. For once in my life, I made some friends...

Punished! Grounded. No witchcraft for one month!

But, Mom...

In the end, he was a victim.

Poor kid, well-behaved.

Pff.

Let's go, Super Club. My parents are waiting.

51

Lola's SUPER CLUB

"MY GRAMPY IS THE KING OF SPORTS"

ONE OLD-TIMEY GOAL LATER...

So, all fixed up?

Come on in...

There's the King of Sports!

Careful, c'mere...

Pass me the remote, my Lola!

The race is ending...

Right away, Grampy!

What an incredible finish to this fantastic journey around the world in 80 days--

Ah, shut your trap!

Click!

Yellow's gaining...

Who's that?

I know him!

Turn it up, Grampy!

Nice, Boss!

Boss, nice!

That's my son!

... the big winner of this last desert leg. He did the maximum to surpass the scorching 150 degree breeze... in the shade!

Quiet, Guillermo! You fool!

Rats! I smell a trap!

Click!

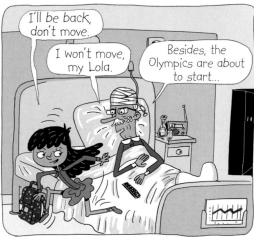

I'll be back, don't move.

I won't move, my Lola.

Besides, the Olympics are about to start...

Hurry up, my Lola!

Zap!

The Olympics? The Super Club can't miss that!

It's time for a new adventure! If I can get there...

There! That works...

CRiiiiiii

Super Club! No sleeping on the job!

WAOOF

Ziiiiiiii

FLUCH

???

Exceptional. This year the Games last a short time so the Organization has prepared new events. Let's keep it sporty.

In fact, the Organization is here next to me. The mix of challenges will be a riot, right, Mini Love?

No doubt, dear Guinemo!

Let's start with the triple obstacle jump with a pole vault!

Could you walk us through this, my Mini-dearest?

It's easy. A triple jump to reach the baton there. Yes, quite tall. Then, clear the bar with a pole vault without touching it...

Magnificent, Sweetie...

I'm not done, ingrate!

After that, you must do a freestyle jump to the finish. That's it.

Fascinating! Remember, each competitor has two tries.

And here's our first competitor... Friendly Fall's Super-Gator! He jumps, one, two, three... Will he make it...? Yes! He does and-- Oops!

POC POC POC

The pole seems particularly heavy for JUNGLOR who's more used to vines. He aims towards the shaking baton, and... fail!

So close!

SPLASH

Second and last try for Junglor, who does his famous cry... throws the pole and... welp, say bye to Junglor.

Oooooo... IIIIIIII...

CRAC SPLASH

Owww!

Nyuk!

Super Club, step aside! Vlad Dracula from Fiendish Falls enters the field. Will he fare better than his adversaries?

Duh! Vampires sink their teeth into sports! And he's off and--

Blind as a bat!

OUCH

To the victor goes the spoils! What a dive! Vlad nailed the leap with agility, cooked the croc, double corkscrew, and bamboozled the finish line. How many points, Judge Mini?

POC

SPLASH

One hundred!

Here comes the triple-whatsit master: Max Imum! Oh! It seems he has grasshoppers in his shoes! But no, his fat makes him float ...

Float, idiot! You hop over the bar at 400 meters and execute a dangerous dolphin leap, with a shark-tip dive into the drink! Go faster! Maxi Boom! Pow! That's worth 1,000 points...

SPLASH

Second try. He takes off and...Ooooh! Aaaah! Yes! A Backwards Shark Fin Spin, with a very nice rush this time! That's not all, folks: The Angry Koala Stance, Sea Lion Slip, a Butterfly Umbrella Stroke and...

BING

VROOOO

...for the dive, he's as graceful as a walrus. Not too much splash. Bravo! That's my boy!

Ahem! Sweetie, let's decide the score. And it's the...maximum! He's pulverized all records! 10,000 points! Max Champ!

Thanks, Mommy, love you!

Paging the studio, you're still live! Hello? Anyone there?

Event 2

UPHILL MARTIAL ARTS

Ahem! Yes. While our champ celebrates, uphill martial arts qualifiers weeded out the weak, who've been brought to nearby hospitals.

Nyuk!

TS

Now, meet the finalists of the finals, who are... uh... uh... Umm, who are they?

There's only two of them, fool!

PRESS BOX   PRESS BOX   PR

Right! Super-James with dumb flowers on his undies and...

BRAVO

CLAP
CLAP

Rocky Ogre! Grrr, we're fans!

CLAP   CLAP
CLAP

Let's go! The first to arrive at the top of the mountain...

Alive...

Yes, alive, first to arrive wins...

BANG

66

Viewers, we continue these wild, wild games with track and pool, which starts with the arrival of the swimmers...

Just introduce the teams.

TRACK AND POOL

The electric medusas: Max Imum, Zombi-Zomba, Wolf Man, and Robotoc.

The Super Fishsticks: Lola, Momina the scribble monster, Skeletina, and Shark.

The villains prepare for the 50 meter hurdle. Go. Dead silence rings over the crowd...

SPLASH SPLASH SPLASH SPLASH

GLUB GLOB GBULÉ

They're off as Michael Jackson's music fills the pool ...

Because I'm bad, I'm bad...

The Super Fishsticks are ready to dive despite the floundering of the villains.

Poor sportsmanship. How cruel, Friendly Falls!

Happy birthday...

SPLASH

SPLASH

Happy birthday

Oh, it's your birthday?

Of course not, it's their music.

Happy birthday...

Happy birthday...

Interesting first jump!

Bah... easy.

To you...

Happy birthday to-- Ow! Sweetie!

BONG

BONG

Happy birthday...

Dear Super Club...

Good show!

:Pff.:

73

Seems like the games have taken a turn for the worse, huh, Baby?

BIKING-CANOE-KAYAK- ARCHERY- PLUNGE

Exactly, dearie. And the worse will get worst with the next event...

Friendly Falls has chosen ROBIN GOOD and his rain-bow, James and Lola on pedals.

For us, Maxi-bullseye will do the shooting, while the useless ones will pedal nonstop. That they can do...I hope.

Here's the first curve... and it looks like it's gonna rain!

A rain of arrows, dearie, pouring on the Super Club...

Now, James! Grow!

And you, Sir Robin, shoot! Aim for the fat mustached guy!

Did you hear, Boss? She said you had a fat mus--

Shut up! Shut up!

Did you see the growy guy, Boss? It's a trap!

IN THE HEAT OF THESE EVILYMPICS GAMES, THE MORALE OF THE FRIENDLY FALLS TEAM IS ON THE FLOOR... MORE LIKE IN THE BASEMENT...

No fair!

You said it, Super-Gator, but I know who can help us regroup.

Who?

Hey, Grampy? Can you walk? We need you in Malbar!

And? What'd he say?

He said: "On my way, my Lola. Leaving the hospital and taking the first bus."

Momina, turn on the TV and find a medical show!

BZiiP

Hot Dog, open the book!

Will "ER" do?

Bam! Volume #1!

Nice! Momina, you zap it, Hot Dog, hold up the cover.

SPLICH

Hey, kids! What's happening?

80

Good! It's time to re-train your feet and your heads!

Getting down in the dumps is off-limits!

Besides, you're quite clean, so no dumps...

Funny face-off!

Jump on the bed! It's a pillow fight!

Close your eyes and listen up. Games, even the Evilympics, are still just games. The point is to have fun.

Perfect. We can do it together. Happy and in a good mood.

Who's the strongest?

THE SUPER CLUB!

IN THE FIENDISH FALLS CLUBHOUSE, THINGS ARE DIFFERENT...

You sunk in the kiddie pool and you got smacked by the waves! You useless worthless bunch!

But Mommy, we're winning!

SPLASH

Not good enough, we must crush them.

Like this!

Quit being weaklings! We won't let the Super Club score one point! No more caca.

What are you doing, Max?

You said no more caca...

You disgust me. Move your butt!

Yes, Mommy, going, Mommy!

You'll see! You won't lose with this potion. Guinemo, do you have the ingredients?

Yes, Love. Here you are.

Asterix has his potion and now so do you.

It'll be delicious, I'm telling you!

PLUF PLOK PLUC

There. Who wants it?

BLUB BLUB BLUB

Guinemo?

Why always me? Besides, I should concentrate on my sports announcer commentary, Honey.

For once, you're right. Here, Max, open up for Mom...

SLURP

Hiiii!

Don't worry, there's enough for all. Not you, Guinemo... Get in line!

Dear viewersh, after this shmall pause we can re-commence the feshtivities. It's time for ping pong with way--wait--way...

Weightlifting! I hope you didn't drink the potion, my thirsty duck...

Me? ؛Hic!؛ No.

Jungle Junglor will face the very vampire-y Vlad Dracula. Will they get past the first task, lifting the deadweight of dog bonesh?

WEIGHTLIFTING PING PONG

The two athletesh are off to a good shtart and they're lifting their shtuff...

WEIGHTLIFTING PING PONG

Wow, what a bat! Vlad almost pinged a pong... Ping?

Not yet, watch. Well played, Zero. For once...

PING

PONG

PONG

And ؛hic؛, first win. Friendly Falls has the smasht.

It's not over, rematch!

PONG

PONG

PONG

Second batch. This time the vill-⇒hic⇐-ains got this in the bag.

Oh! Reversal pass from Zero..!

It's called "Match," dope!

Junglor and the skeletons are very coornibrated ⇒hic⇐ coordinated...

So what? Go on, Zeros, be heroes for once!

PONG

PING

Turn to the right!

No, I'll go left!

Pick one...

PONG

The bad guys got some bad blood. Oh! I'm funny, Toots... ⇒Hic!⇐

Lame...

A bone-crusher from miss Skele-⇒Hic!⇐-ton. Then Drac ducks, steps on his cape and steps in it!

Shut up, just shut up...

OOHIHOHIHOOOO... HIHOHIHAAAA!

Those villains, ⇒hic,⇐ lose the bing bong smasht!

MAAATCH! MATCH! MATCH! MATCH!

BONG

Ah! That felt good. Let's rig the next event, shall we?

Yes, Baby. Did I say that okay? Ah! No more hiccups...

The big guy in undies and the super-purse wont do better than the villains, no way!

Go ahead, Super-Gator! Bon voyage.

No fair!

No faaairr!

Ow! Uff! Ouch, ouch...

Be brave, you're almost there!

Still alive? Ready for the final throw?

No fair!

Alley-oop.

There!

WZIiii

See you later, Gator!

How can that be?

YOU BIG DUMMY!

BONG

RYTHMIC EQUESTRIAN

Now up in the arena, Rythmic Equestrian. On one side, a Hot Dog riding a Super-Chump and the other...Glutboog on top of the ferocious Wolf Man!

The wolf is hot to trot...

The ribbons dazzle...

Admire our favorite booger...

Boogie down!

Go team!

They forgot their apparatus. Super.

Finally!

Bah...

The horse thinks he's a monkey.

Mmm?

Uh. How? Now?

ARTISTIC OBSTACLE JUMP

It's upside down! Hurry, we're starting!

ARTISTIC OBSTACLE JUMP

ARTISTIC OBSTACLE JUMP

3, 2, 1, my son won!

Yee-haw! Warm up, Dragon!

PSHiiii

Asymmetrical twirl.

Super-Grampy!

Take it away, Momina!

So, bag witch... Yay or neigh?

Stop-watch is busted.

Well, fine... 5 points to each team!

A tie?! Let me see that, you must be wrong...

Events	Villains vs Super Club
Triple Obstacle Jump with a Pole Vault	
Uphill Martial Arts	V
Track and Pool	V
Surfing Fencing	S
Dodgeboat	S
Biking-Canoe-Kayak	S
Archery-Plunge	V
Weightlifting Ping Pong	V
Shot Put-Basketball-Golf	S
Rythmic Equestrian	S
Artistic Obstacle Jump	V
42,195 Piece Puzzle Marathon	S
TOTAL POINTS	5 to 5

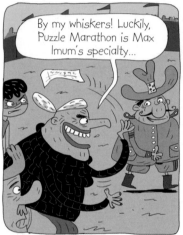

By my whiskers! Luckily, Puzzle Marathon is Max Imum's specialty...

Dear viewers, we remind you there's 42,195 pieces in this muzzle.

Puzzle!

42,195 PIECE PUZZLE MARATHON

On three, the race begins.

Nyuk, anything goes, now...

THREEE!

Look! I got a ton of them!

No fair!

TEN HOURS LATER...

Run, Max Imum!

Go, go, go, go!

Done!

Done!

It's a tie.

SLAP

Here, Lola!

Too late, we have the baton for victory!

We haven't lost yet!

Go, Super-Lola! Run, fly, avenge us!

Mummy's wraps! We're zombie meat now!

Cut them!

Problem, Maxy?

Claimed the win too soon, eh?

Fasterrr!

Almosgosit!

Do something, Mommy! Help!

Abracadobra, legs like cobra!

Ziuiuiu

Ow, my legs feel like jelly, Grampy!

Leave it to the King of Sports... Hang on, Lola!

When legs don't work, we need to use our heads and... run with our arms!

First!

Super-Grampy!

You're the best!

⸸SOB!⸷

99

And so, that's how the Evilympic Games end, with a Friendly win over the villains... Signing off, I'm going to drown my sorrows with my team.

EVILYMPIC GAMES - MALBAR ISLANDS
FIRST PLACE WINNERS: FRIENDLY FALLS

1

⸭Waaaaah!⸭ We lo-lo-lost...

⸭Grrr!⸭ Quit blubbering, you big baby... You're hopeless!

⸭Snif!⸭ They could've let me win for once! How unfriendly! How fiendish, you villains! Bad, bad villains!

Us? Never. Did you forget? The Club of Villains is you guys...

And as we are good, we decided to share the chocolate medals.

R-really?

Of course not, fool. Can't you see she's trying to trick you?

Don't listen to her, Max. The spellcasting witch is your mom, not me!

Curses! I'll shut that trap.

Sweetie, no! Sportmanship is in the rules.

Yes, for once listen to Guimemo: accept your loss with sportsmanship!

BONG

Mommy!

My Mini Love! It's me, Guillermo, your prince, your favorite dearie... Can you hear me?

You knocked out my mom?! You'll pay for that!

Uh-oh, I think now is a good time to head home, my Lola...

Yeah, the competition stinks.

Retreat, Super Club! Everyone in Guinemo's balloon!

Trampolimomin!

Faster, Gator!

I thought we were done with sports for today. No fair!

♪Uff.♪ That was close...

And now, how do we get back?

The radio frequency, Grampy... Radio Friendly Falls, remember it?

Ah, this! Why didn't you say so? Channel 96 FM.

Radiomomina!

4 PM and you're listening to Radio Friendly Falls. Ah, 4, snack time!

In you go!

Time to get rolling, Mister Darkhair.

No problem, Miss. I won a gold medal in wheelchair racing...

Good one! And I'm the Queen of Friendly Falls!

You won the medal for Best Grampy in Friendly Falls and the Whole World and of All Time too!

Ah, my Lola! Friendliness is a daily event, never forget.

You got it, Grampy!

EXIT

RENE TOUILLET 2020

WATCH OUT FOR PAPERCUTZ™

Welcome to LOLA'S SUPER CLUB #2 "My Substitute Teacher is a Witch" by Christine Beigel and Pierre Fouillet from Papercutz—those superlative sentient beings dedicated to publishing great graphic novels for all ages. I'm Jim Salicrup, the Editor-in-Chief and Max Imum's mustache consultant, here to offer some possible insights into one of the possible inspirations for some of the craziness found within this sophomoric volume of LOLA'S SUPER CLUB...

I'm beginning to suspect that LOLA'S SUPER CLUB creators are fans of ASTERIX, the classic series created by René Goscinny, writer, and Albert Uderzo, illustrator. After all, ASTERIX is one of the biggest selling comics series in the whole world, even though most Americans are still unaware of ASTERIX. Well, that's about to change because I'm proud to say that Papercutz (that's us!) has just recently become the American publisher of this classic comics property. And that's not all. It was recently announced that an animated ASTERIX limited series is being developed right now for NetFlix. It won't be available for a couple of years, but that just gives you plenty of time to read all the ASTERIX stories being collected in every volume of ASTERIX from Papercutz. By the time the animated series debuts, you'll know all about ASTERIX.

But why did I suspect the creators of LOLA'S SUPER CLUB to be fans of ASTERIX? Well, remember in LOLA'S SUPER CLUB #1 there was this: When Lola landed in 50 BC, some of you may have gotten the inside gag based on one of the best-selling comics series in the world, ASTERIX. That's the comic Lola refers to when she says, "to defeat the Romans you must drink a magic potion." And speaking of that magic potion, check out page 83 in this volume of LOLA'S SUPER CLUB, where Mini-Mum says to her partner, "Asterix has his potion and now so do you," as she hands him her cauldron of pure yuckiness.

So, who is this ASTERIX fellow that Christine and Pierre keep mentioning? To answer that we need to journey back to the year 50 BC in the ancient country of Gaul, located where France, Belgium, and the Southern Netherlands are today. All of Gaul has been conquered by the Romans... well, not all of it. One tiny village, inhabited by indomitable Gauls, resists the invaders again and again. That doesn't make it easy for the garrisons of Roman soldiers surrounding the village in fortified camps.

So, how's it possible that a small village can hold its own against the mighty Roman Empire? The answer is this guy...

This is **Asterix**. A shrewd, little warrior of keen intellect... and superhuman strength. Asterix gets his superhuman strength from a magic potion. But he's not alone.

Obelix is Asterix's inseparable friend. He too has superhuman strength. He's a menhir (tall, upright stone monuments) deliveryman, he loves eating wild boar and getting into brawls. Obelix is always ready to drop everything to go off on a new adventure with Asterix.

Panoramix, the village's venerable Druid, gathers mistletoe and prepares magic potions. His greatest success is the power potion. When a villager drinks this magical elixir he or she is temporarily granted super-strength. This is just one of the Druid's potions! And now you know why this small village can survive, despite seemingly impossible odds. There are plenty more characters in ASTERIX, and you can meet them by picking up any volume of ASTERIX available now at your favorite bookseller or library.

There's also another Papercutz super-hero we want to tell you about. His graphic novel series is just as wacky, if not more so than LOLA'S SUPER CLUB. The series is called ASTRO MOUSE AND LIGHT BULB, created by Fermín Solís, and we suspect you'll like it just as much as LOLA. Just check out the preview starting on the next page and see for yourself. Now that you have ASTERIX and ASTRO MOUSE AND LIGHT BULB to enjoy, don't forget about the next volume of LOLA'S SUPER CLUB, coming soon to that same bookseller or library that you like so much. Face it, there's never a dull moment when you're enjoying a Papercutz graphic novel—but it's no fun without you!

Thanks,

STAY IN TOUCH!

EMAIL: salicrup@papercutz.com
WEB: papercutz.com
TWITTER: @papercutzgn
INSTAGRAM: @papercutzgn
FACEBOOK: PAPERCUTZGRAPHICNOVELS
FAN MAIL: Papercutz, 160 Broadway,
Suite 700, East Wing
New York, NY 10038
Go to papercutz.com and sign up for the free e-newsletter!

Now, for an out of this world preview of ASTRO MOUSE AND LIGHT BULB #1

ASTRO MOUSE AND LIGHT BULB #1 © 2021 Fermín Solís

Astro Mouse and Light Bulb have met their mash! Find out what happens in ASTRO MOUSE AND LIGHT BULB #1 available now wherever books are sold!